GRANDMA DRIVES A MOTOR BED

GRANDMA DRIVES A MOTOR BED

Diane Johnston Hamm

pictures by Charles Robinson

ALBERT WHITMAN & COMPANY, NILES, ILLINOIS

Library of Congress Cataloging-in-Publication Data

Hamm, Diane Johnston.
Grandma drives a motor bed.

Summary: Josh and his grandmother share happy times together although illness confines her to a motor-driven bed.
[1. Grandmothers—Fiction. 2. Physically handicapped—Fiction] I. Robinson, Charles, 1931- ill. II Title.
PZ7.H1837Gr 1987 [E] 87-2197
ISBN 0-8075-3025-5

Designed by Margit Wevang Leavitt

Published in 1987 by Albert Whitman & Company, Niles, Illinois
Published simultaneously in Canada by General Publishing, Limited, Toronto

10 9 8 7 6 5 4 3 2 1

For Mom and Dad *D.J.H.*
For Mimi *C.R.*

It takes five hours for Mama and me to get to Grandma's house. That's my grandma who drives a motor bed. She can make her bed go up and down with a control box.

One button makes just the top sit up. Another raises Grandma's feet.

"The only thing my motor bed won't do is wash the dishes," Grandma says.

When I first saw that bed I said, “Where’s the motor?”

“Why don’t you crawl underneath and find out?” Grandma said.

All I could see under there was a long box with cords sticking out. It started to make a “rrr-rrr” sound. The bed was moving! “Hey, Grandma, don’t squish me!” I called.

“Don’t worry,” she said. “This bed is going up.”

Every time I visit I want to try that bed out myself.

But Grandma's almost always in it. That's because her legs don't work. She can't even get up to go to the bathroom.

She wears throw-away diapers. I hold my breath when I first go into her room. Sometimes it smells like a bathroom in there.

Mostly Grandpa takes care of Grandma.

But when he goes downtown, Grandma takes care of herself. She has her own telephone, a radio, a TV, and lots of books.

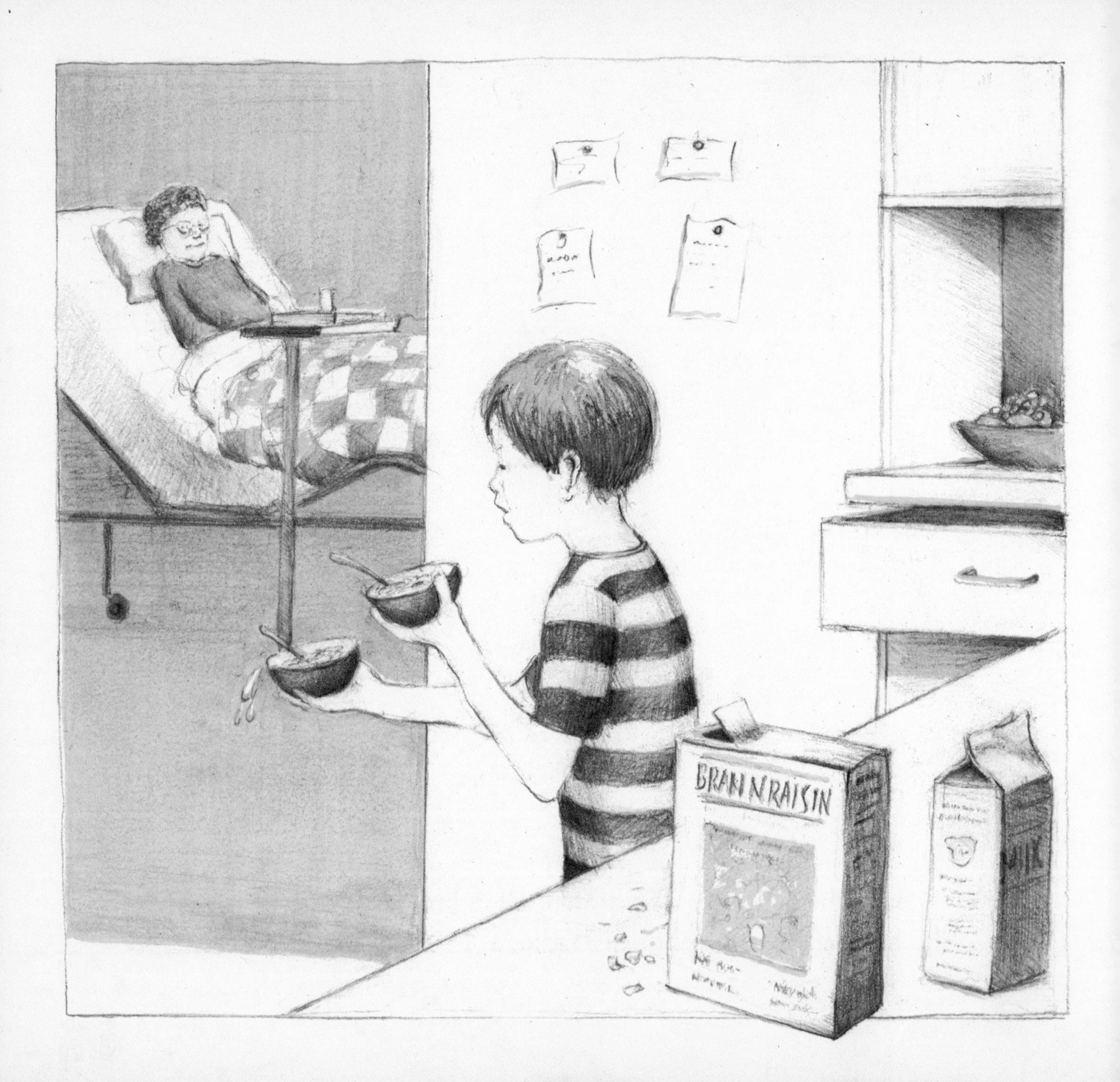
BRAN N RAISIN
MILK

When I come I help, too. I bring Grandma candy from the cupboard. I fill her water glass. And in the morning when no one else is up, I bring her a bowl of raisin bran.

When Grandma has energy, she likes to write letters. Yesterday she said, "Josh, let's send a note to your Uncle Dan. He hasn't been able to find a job."

I got to push the forward button so Grandma could sit straight up. Mama brought the typewriter.

"We could tell Uncle Dan to stay out of trouble," I said.

Sometimes it takes Grandma and me two days to finish a letter.

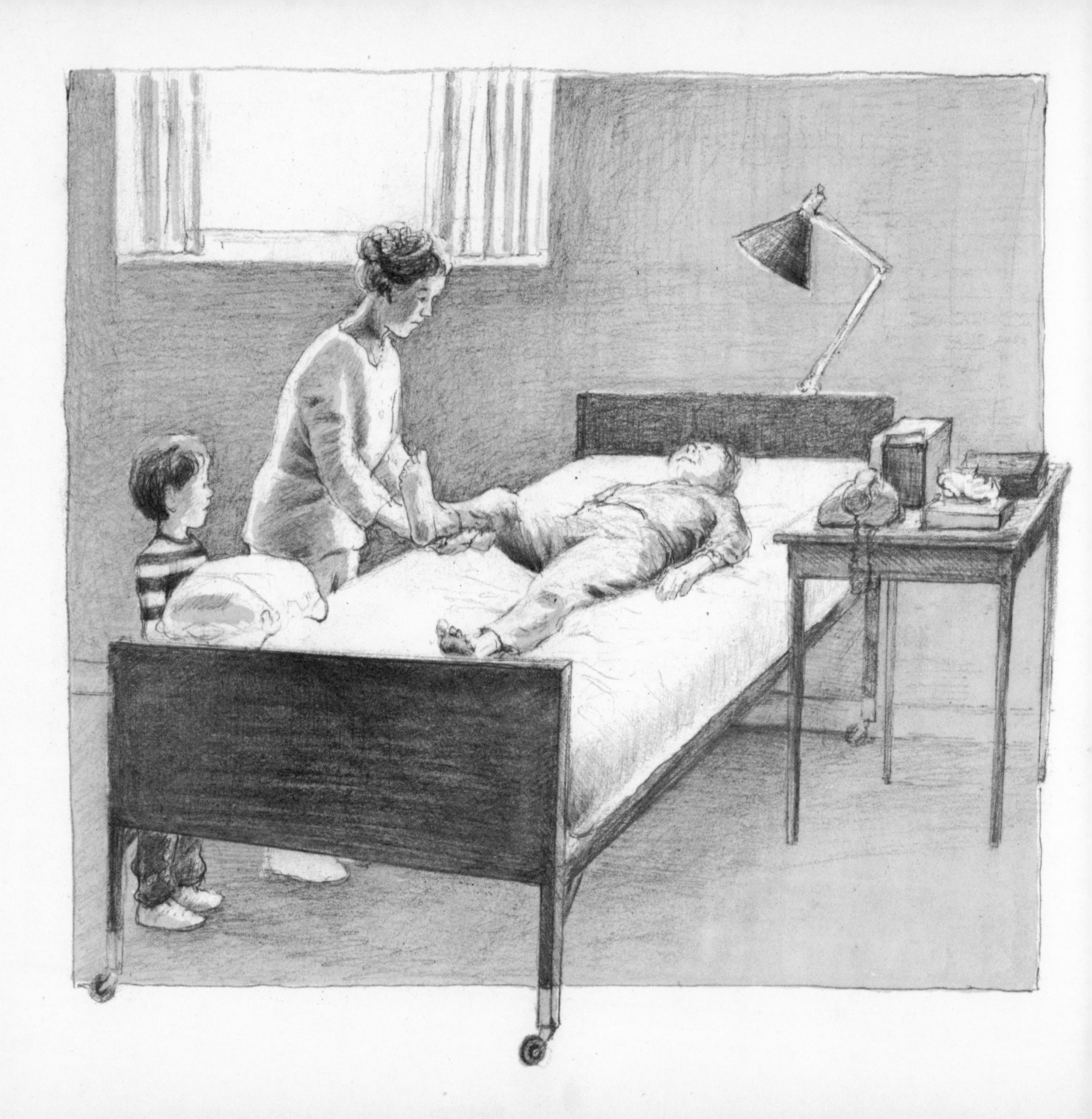

Some days a helper comes after lunch to do exercises with Grandma. She lifts Grandma's arms and legs and makes her roll her head. "I don't want to get flabby muscles," Grandma tells me.

And some days Grandma has lots of visitors. They tell her their troubles. They laugh, too.

Mama said Grandma gives them courage. She never complains to them about being in bed.

This morning Grandma was sad. She knows Mama and I have to go home tomorrow. She said, "Josh, I wish you lived closer. There are many days when people don't have time to visit. No letters come, either.

"I'd like to call you on the phone then. I'd say, 'Come over for tea and cookies and tell me what you're up to.' "

Grandma looked like she needed a hug. I gave her one. "Oh, how I wish these legs worked," she said real quietly. "Sometimes, I feel like I'm never going to get better."

Mama told me maybe Grandma will get better and maybe she won't. Nobody knows.

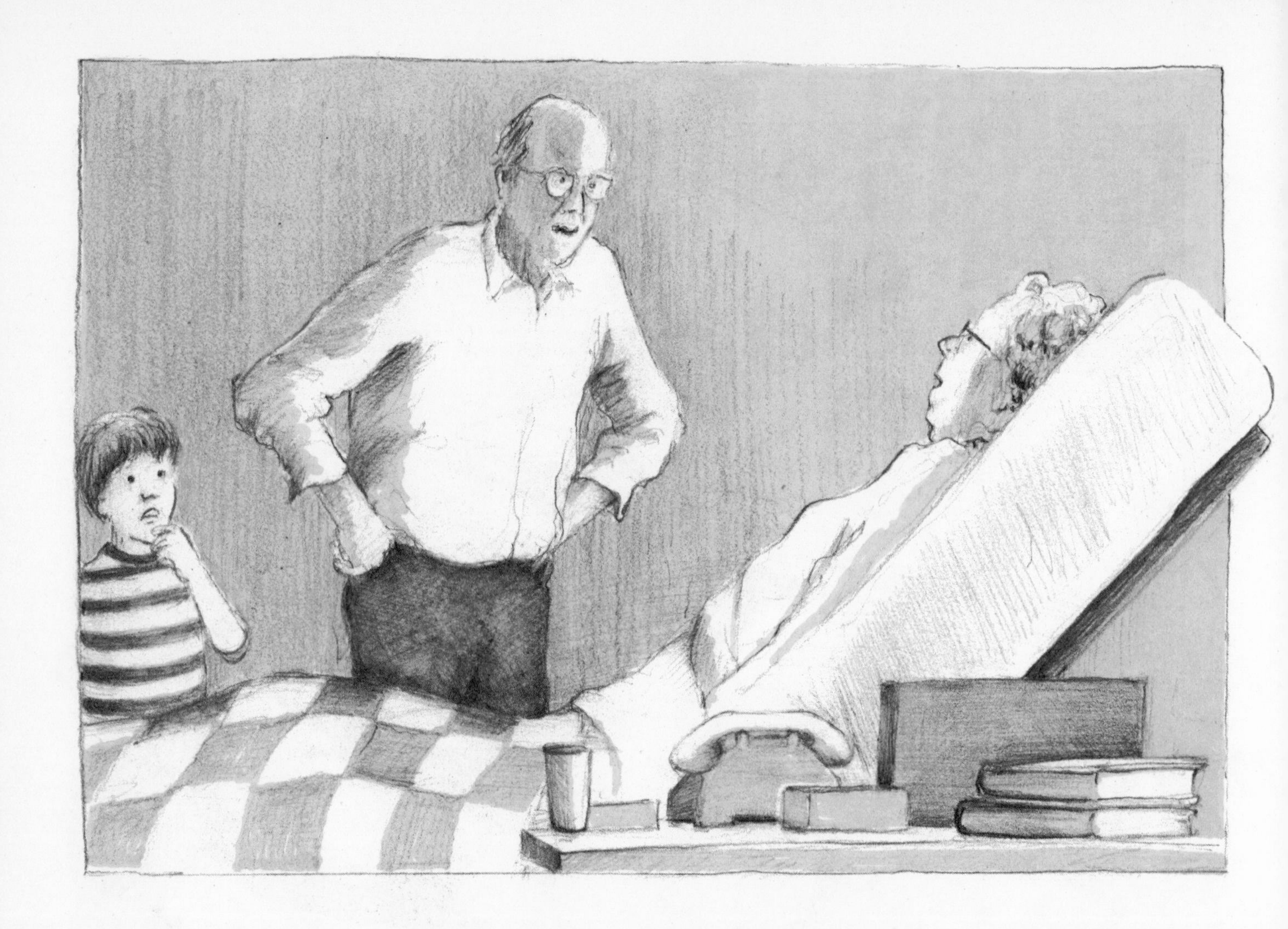

Last time I came to visit, Grandpa hollered at Grandma. I was scared. Mama said, “Listen, Josh, even grandparents get frustrated and grumpy. Grandpa loves Grandma very much.”

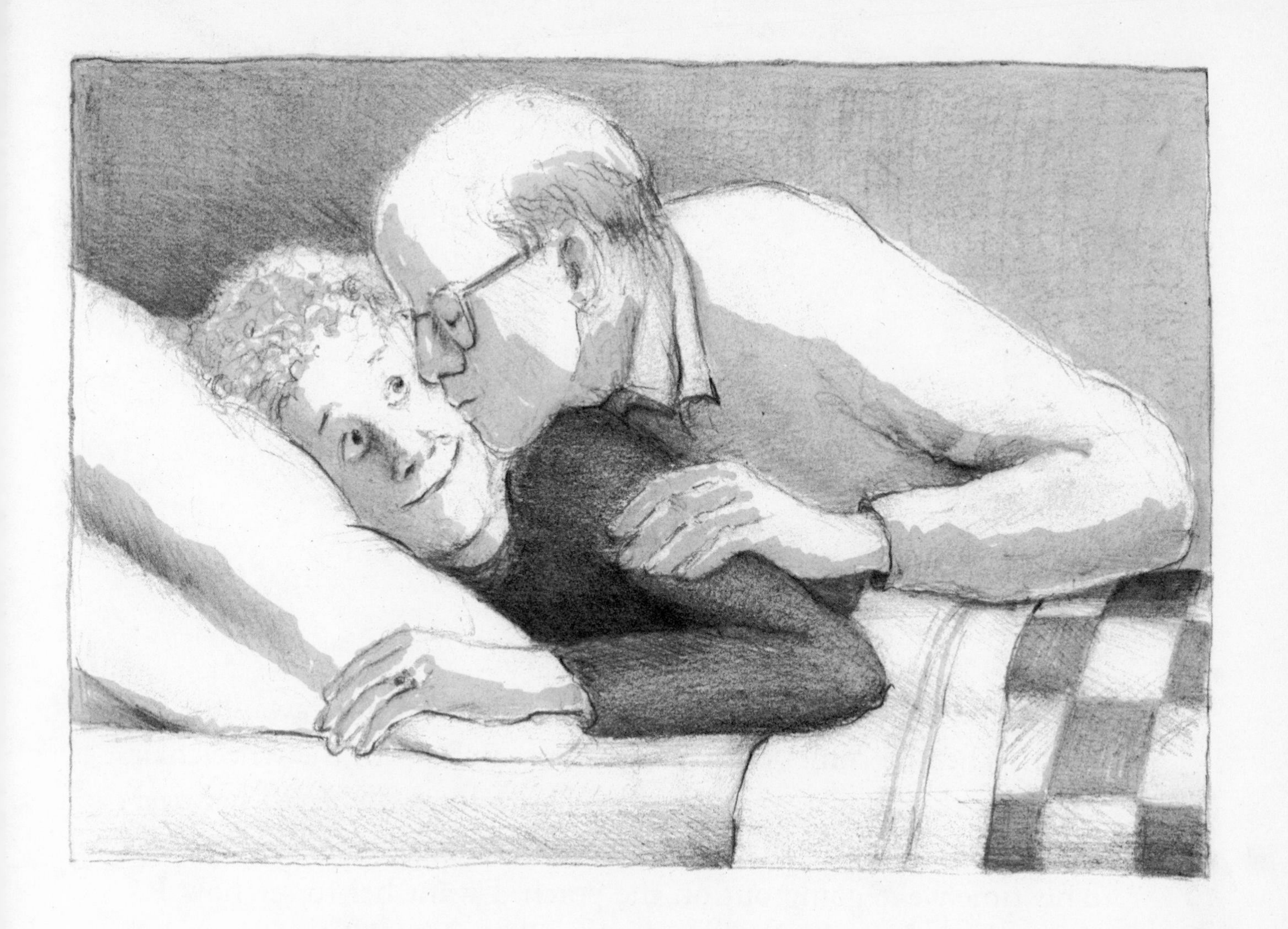

I think it must be true. Grandma's eyes get all shiny at night when Grandpa gives her a back rub. He nibbles on her ear and she says, "Oh, Harold."

Sometimes when Mama and I are here, Grandpa goes away for a vacation. When he comes back, we get Grandma up in the wheelchair.

She likes that, but it wears her out. Last winter I wheeled her over to the fireplace. She said that was a nice little vacation for her.

This time we're going out on the porch. I want her to see how I can swing high enough to touch the branches now. When I come again, the swing might be too small for me.

"How clever you are to get yourself higher than last time," Grandma tells me, just like she always does.

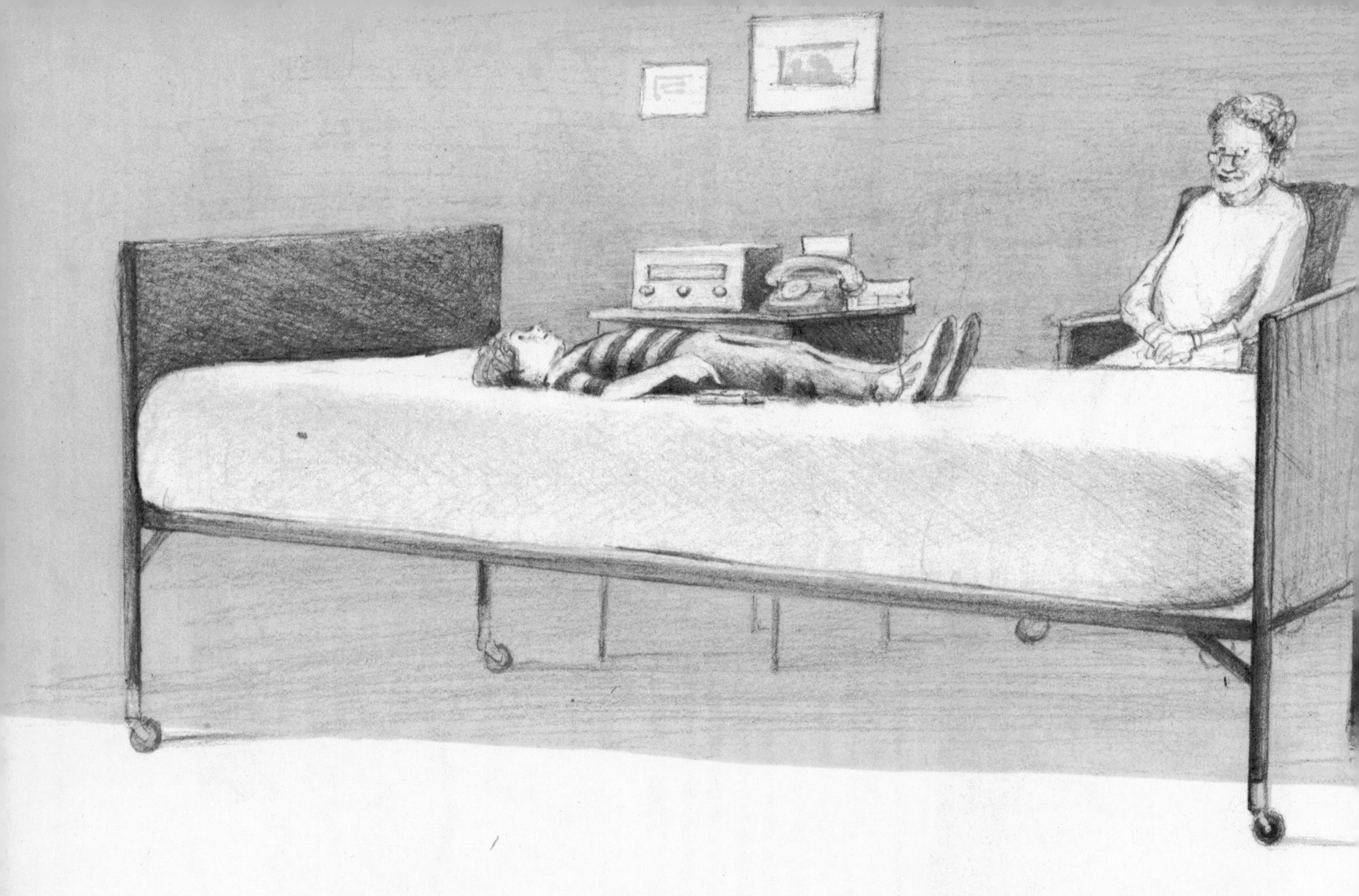

When I bring Grandma back in, she says, "Josh, my bed doesn't seem to be working properly. Why don't you hop up real quick and see what you think?"

"You mean try it out?" I say. "You bet, Grandma!" I don't even take off my shoes.

I find the control box and get into position. "Up." I push.

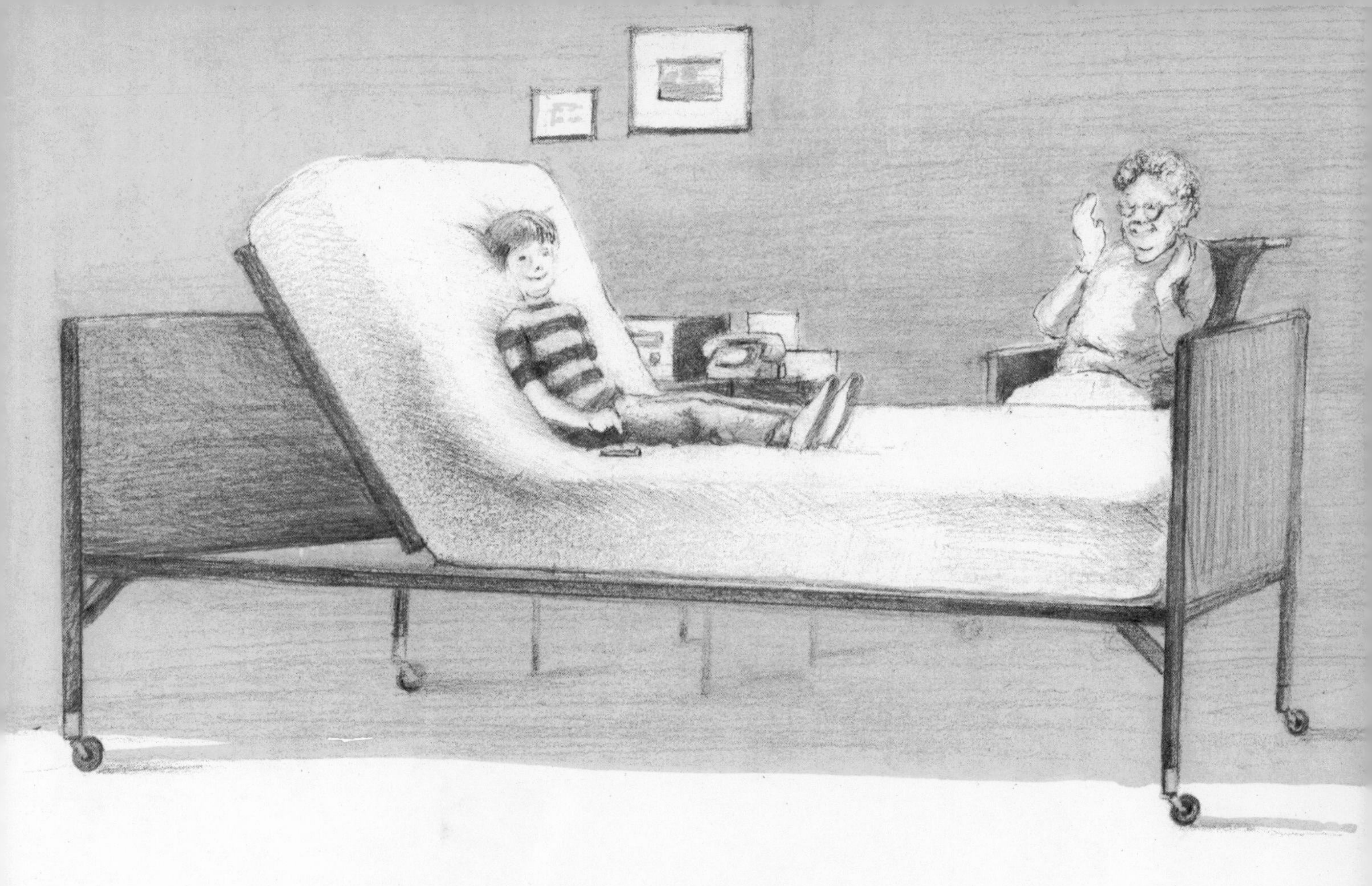

"Rrr-rrr." The bed is a giant's hand lifting me into the air.

"Down," I say. Lower and lower the bed goes. I tell Grandma, "It's a little slow going down."

Then the middle button. Slowly, slowly, I'm sitting up! Slowly, slowly, back down. Next the button for the feet. H-e-r-e they come.

"It seems to be working fine, Grandma, just a little slow."

"Good," says Grandma. "These motor beds ought to be tested out from time to time."

She winks at me. "Now jump down and let me have a turn."